THE
LITTLE JEWEL BOX

by *Marianna Mayer* · *pictures by Margot Tomes*

DIAL BOOKS FOR YOUNG READERS : *New York*

Published by Dial Books for Young Readers
2 Park Avenue
New York, New York 10016
A Division of E. P. Dutton
A Division of New American Library
Published simultaneously in Canada
by Fitzhenry and Whiteside Limited, Toronto
Design by Atha Tehon
Printed in Hong Kong by South China Printing Co.
First Edition
COBE
10 9 8 7 6 5 4 3 4 2 1

Library of Congress Cataloging-in-Publication Data

Mayer, Marianna.
The little jewel box.
Summary: Cursed with bad luck, a courageous young girl sets
out in search of adventure, her only protection a little jewel box
that she is to open only when in danger of death.
[1. Fairy tales.] I. Tomes, Margot, ill. II. Title.
PZ8.M4514Li 1986. [E] 85-16003
ISBN 0-8037-0148-9
ISBN 0-8037-0149-7 (lib. bdg.)

The full-color artwork was prepared in gouache.
It was then camera-separated and reproduced
in red, blue, yellow, and black halftones.

For Valerie and Samantha Leonard M. M.

For Jacqueline M. T.

Once upon a time, not in my time or your time, but a very long time ago, a young girl named Isabel lived with her mother and father on a quiet farm in the country. Isabel loved to read books, and since she had no brothers or sisters or friends her own age, she would amuse herself by imagining that she was the heroine of every tale she read.

As time passed, Isabel made plans about what she would do once she grew up. Perhaps she would fight dragons or discover new lands or rescue the helpless from danger. So convinced was Isabel that she would be brave and true to her purpose, whatever it might turn out to be, that she felt no difficulty would be impossible to conquer.

At last she decided to go out into the world to seek adventure. But Isabel's parents were horrified when she told them.

"That's impossible!" they exclaimed. "It's much too dangerous."

But Isabel didn't believe anything was impossible. She insisted and insisted until finally her parents agreed to let her go.

Her mother set about making a good luck cake as a parting gift for her journey. However, the poor woman was so upset at the idea of her only child going into the world that she read the wrong recipe from the cookbook and made a bad luck cake instead. Neither Isabel nor her mother were any the wiser when Isabel took the bad luck cake, and with many kisses, said good-bye.

Next Isabel went to say good-bye to her father. All the night before he had thought about a gift for his daughter. Finally he decided that she should have the little jewel box his grandmother had given him long ago.

Kissing Isabel good-bye, he said, "If you're ever in danger of death you must open the box, but not till then. It has been in our family for generations, but since we have lived quietly in the woods, we have never had the need to use it."

Isabel thanked her father for the jewel box and soon was on her way.
She traveled all that day and at twilight she stopped to rest. As she was
eating the cake her mother had made her, she saw a large house in the dis-
tance and decided to go there to ask for lodging.

John, the master's son, let her in and gave her a cup of hot tea. After talking to Isabel for a time, he decided she was quite the most interesting person he had ever met. Here was a girl who was brave, outspoken, and intelligent besides. He felt certain he had fallen in love with her already.

John immediately went to his father and announced that he intended to marry Isabel. But the master didn't like this at all. He thought, "Why should my son marry a perfect stranger when there are so many wealthy girls nearby who would love to have him." However, he did not wish to make his son angry, so he decided to meet Isabel and ask her what work she could do.

"Anything at all," answered Isabel happily; she was only too glad to work for her lodging. Besides it would give her a chance to get to know John better, for she liked him very much indeed.

But unfortunately Isabel's bad luck cake had already begun to do its work. Suddenly the master saw a way of appearing to grant his son's wish but really to get rid of Isabel instead.

"Well, my girl," he said quickly, "if you can do anything at all, then do this: By seven o'clock tomorrow morning you must dig up the barren field behind my house. And there you must create a magnificent garden with fragrant flowers. Let us have exotic birds besides with songs lovely enough to wake my son who always oversleeps."

Isabel was shocked. "And what if I can't?" she asked.

"Then, my dear," the master said calmly, "you must forfeit your life, that is, *if* you are still here tomorrow."

After bowing low to Isabel, he led her to the tower room where she was to spend the night, *if* she wished to remain.

Once Isabel was alone, she walked to the window, trying to think what she should do. Should she leave in the middle of the night like a coward, or should she stay and try to think of a solution to the master's demands? But she was so tired that at last she shrugged her shoulders, crawled into bed, and promptly went to sleep.

In the morning Isabel awoke with a start and rushed to the window. The field remained barren. Not one flower bloomed and not a single bird sang. Then she looked at the clock tower. To her horror, it was just seconds before seven o'clock and the clock had already begun to strike. One, two, three…All at once, Isabel remembered the little jewel box. "I suppose I'm near enough to death to open it," she thought.

No sooner had she lifted the lid then out popped three extraordinary little men in blue-and-white striped pajamas with matching nightcaps, rubbing their eyes and yawning loudly.

They were quite startled to be called upon, for it had been years and years since anyone had needed them. Between elaborate yawns they asked, "What do you wish, mistress?"

Isabel heard the clock striking. Four, five…Knowing she didn't have a second to lose, she quickly told them what she needed.

Without another word the three little men flew from the window. Six, seven…Suddenly there was a great symphony of birds. Isabel looked out the window and saw the most beautiful garden imaginable. Flowers of every color were blooming and songbirds sang in the trees. Their music was so sweet that John immediately awoke and came to his window. Filled with admiration for Isabel, he smiled and waved happily to her.

Isabel was so transfixed by the sight of the wonderful garden that she jumped when the three little men returned. They flew past her in a flurry and scrambled into the jewel box. "Miss, give us a bit more notice should you be so unfortunate as to need us again, *please*!" they grumbled as they pulled down the lid with a bang. Isabel could hear them yawning inside the box as they settled down to rest.

Even though clever Isabel had fulfilled her task, the master was still not willing to agree to the wedding. He and John went to see Isabel and the master said, "My son wishes to marry you. Will you have him?"

"Oh, yes, I'm quite willing," replied Isabel, smiling at John.

"Indeed," said the master with a frown. "Then you must both have a fine house to live in. Let us look upon it as your dowry. Tomorrow at seven o'clock in the morning, there must be a large castle standing in the new garden with a chapel beside it where you shall be married. But if you fail, you will have to forfeit your life."

Isabel wanted to give the three little men in the jewel box more time to carry out this task, but there was so much celebrating all day long and well into the night that she quite forgot to call on them. In the morning she overslept. The hands on the clock were almost at seven when she leapt from her bed to open the jewel box. But she could not remember where she had hidden it. As the clock began to strike she finally found it under her mattress. With her heart pounding, she opened the box and quickly gave her order.

The three little men flew from the window, dropping their nightcaps, retrieving them, yawning, stretching, and bumping into each other. Four, five, six…This time Isabel thought they would never be able to complete the task. Now she would lose her life for certain! But just as the clock struck seven, chapel bells rang out loudly.

There in the middle of the garden stood a splendid castle with seven brass towers, and next to it was the wedding chapel. Both buildings were hung with wedding decorations, and smiling servants stood waiting for John and Isabel to arrive.

Isabel had never seen anything so grand. She wanted to congratulate the three little men when they returned, but they flew past her without even a "pardon me." They mumbled and grumbled so much about the difficulty she had put them through that Isabel was very relieved when they finally settled into the jewel box, shut the lid with a bang, and began to snore.

Isabel and John were married that day and they lived quite happily for some time. But, though she certainly had every cause to consider herself lucky, the bad luck from her mother's unfortunate cake had not actually worn itself out yet.

One morning when John was still asleep, Isabel went out and forgot to take the jewel box with her. A servant, who had begun to clean her mistress's sitting room, clumsily let the box fall to the floor. The jewel box flew open and out jumped the three little men, stretching and yawning. When they learned they had been summoned only by accident and that there was no danger of death, they became very indignant. "We have a good mind to fly away with this castle, brass towers and all!" they said, fuming.

The servant girl opened her eyes very wide. "Could you actually *do* that?" she asked.

"Why, of course!" they said, laughing mischievously. "We can do anything!"

"Fine. Then move me and this castle to a place far away," ordered the servant girl.

Now there was no real reason for the three little men to obey since the possessor of the jewel box was not near death, but they were still annoyed with Isabel. The servant girl hardly had finished speaking when the chapel, the castle, and everything in it vanished without a trace.

When Isabel returned, she was horrified. Her husband and her home were gone and the jewel box that could have helped her had disappeared too. John's father called her a sorceress and wanted to execute her for the loss of his son.

"Give me three months to make everything right again," said Isabel boldly. "If I fail, I give you my solemn oath I will return and willingly forfeit my life."

"Very well then," he grudgingly agreed. "You have three months, but not a day longer or a minute past seven at night."

Having no time to lose, Isabel saddled a horse and set out immediately. She traveled north and south, east and west, but she never found even the slightest trace of her husband or the castle.

Eventually she came to the palace of the King of All Mice. Standing sentry at the front gate was a tiny mouse riding a large caterpillar; his helmet was a thimble and he had a straight pin for a sword. When Isabel told him her troubles, he felt sorry for her and took her to the King's chambers.

The King of Mice was very gracious. He said he had heard nothing whatsoever about the castle, but he thought that perhaps one of his subjects might know of it. Accordingly he summoned every mouse in his vast domain, but they, too, knew nothing. Then the King told her that she must visit the King of All Frogs, for certainly he would know something more.

As Isabel left the palace gates, she thanked the sentry and gave him some bread. The mouse was so touched by her kindness that he insisted on coming along. When Isabel agreed, he ran up the horse's tail and hid in her right pocket.

After some time, Isabel came to the palace of the King of Frogs. There at the front gate was a frog in tin armor standing guard. The frog was unwilling to let a human into the palace. But when the mouse shouted that they had been sent that very day by the King of Mice, they were quickly ushered into the private rooms of the King. He was very courteous, but he had heard nothing of the castle. He summoned every frog in his domain, but there was not one who knew anything more.

"You must go to my friend the King of All Birds. Perhaps he will be of more help," croaked the King.

Isabel thanked the King and set out again. As she left the gates, she gave the frog wearing tin armor some of her food. The frog was so grateful that he begged to come along. When Isabel agreed, he hopped to the horse's bridle, then to the reins, and at last leapt into her left pocket.

Soon they arrived at the palace of the King of All Birds. There two chickadees marched back and forth guarding the gates. They fluffed their feathers and said they couldn't let a human into the palace. But then the frog and the mouse called out together that they had been sent by their kings so they must be allowed to pass. The chickadees were amazed. Bowing and fluttering, they directed the party to the King's grand hall. The King was a fine old eagle and he welcomed Isabel with much ceremony, but like the others he knew nothing about the missing castle.

All at once Isabel burst into tears. She had not found her beloved John; her time was running out, and soon she must return as she had promised to forfeit her life. Wishing to console her, the eagle ordered every bird in his kingdom to appear, but like the mice and the frogs, none of them could help her. Just as Isabel began to cry again, a hawk flew into the grand hall. He was out of breath from his long journey and his handsome feathers were in disarray. "You're late, Sir Hawk," said the King. "But tell us, have you seen a castle with seven brass towers? This young lady seems to have misplaced it."

"Yes, indeed, your highness. I have just come from there."

Everyone rejoiced at the news. As soon as the hawk had had some food to restore his strength, he spread his wings to carry Isabel, the mouse, and the frog to the castle.

They flew over land and sea until they came to the far-off spot where the castle stood. The sun shone on the beautiful brass towers making them glitter more brilliantly than Isabel remembered. The whole complex, chapel, castle, and all, rested upon a tall hill. The servant girl was out, but she had wisely locked John in before going off with the key. Indeed, everything was barred and shut up tight. They sat down to consider what to do next and the little mouse was the first to speak. "There has not been a castle built that a mouse cannot sneak into," he said proudly.

Isabel told him that if he succeeded he must bring back the little jewel box at once. After he scurried away, the hawk cleaned his feathers nervously, the frog hopped from one webbed foot to the other, and anxious Isabel hummed a song out of tune. But soon the mouse returned with the jewel box balanced on his head.

Isabel breathed a sigh of relief; her time was running short, but now that she had the jewel box, she hoped there was nothing more to worry about. She knew she must wait to open the box at the point that she was truly in danger of death or she might run the risk of having the three little men refuse her. So, putting it safely in her pocket, the small company started back to John's father.

On their way, while passing over a lake, the hawk and the mouse got to quarreling as to who deserved the most credit for helping Isabel. Finally they invited the frog to judge. He said, "I must hear both sides of the tale all over again."

Taking the jewel box from Isabel's pocket, the mouse began to relate how he had found it. But the box slipped from his paws and fell right to the bottom of the lake with a splash!

Everyone shrieked in despair, but the frog laughed and said, "I thought I'd be needed sooner or later." Then he jumped into the lake and disappeared. As they waited desperately, minutes turned to hours.

At nightfall the frog finally popped his head from the water.

"Do you have it?" they asked.

"No," he gasped.

"Then whatever do you want?" they shouted at him.

"Just some air," he answered and sank back into the lake.

Still more time passed, and by dawn up came the frog with the jewel box. Congratulating him happily, they flew off again together.

When they arrived that evening, John's father was not in a welcoming mood. He saw that Isabel had come with a mouse, a frog, and a hawk, but without John or the castle. Exactly three months had passed and the hands of the clock stood just seconds before seven. Indeed, he was quite determined to take her life.

Isabel lifted the lid of the jewel box and out tumbled the three little men. They had got over their anger at her and were quite overjoyed to be back with their true mistress, since the servant girl was forever opening the jewel box and disturbing their sleep when there was no danger of death.

Isabel hoped their good humor would last, for her time was very nearly up. Quickly she told them what was needed. This made the three little men angry all over again. Between yawns and shouts, threats and scolding, they complained. "Fellows shouldn't try to sleep at all! Since we've met you, we've never had a moment's peace!"

In the midst of their tirade the clock in the tower began to strike.

"Gentlemen!" said Isabel, becoming really frightened. "Do as I ask. I *promise* this will be the last time. I will never call upon you again."

This was just what the three little men wanted to hear. "NEVER AGAIN, HA!" they shouted, stamping their feet. "We will not stay with a mistress who is forever getting into scrapes where she must forfeit her life." Setting their nightcaps squarely upon their heads, they flew out the window. Isabel watched them until they were out of sight; she was sure she would not live to see John again, for they had certainly deserted her.

The clock finished striking for the seventh time. It was exactly seven o'clock; the dusky sky was streaked with pink and crimson, and chapel bells were beginning to chime. The joyful sound filled the darkening room as Isabel walked to the window. She made a silent wish that the three little men had helped her one last time. Then she took a deep breath and looked out. There stood the castle, gleaming towers and all! And the bells she heard ringing were from her very own chapel. John was set free. Already he was running to meet her and at last, they lived happily ever after.